TORMENT: A NOVELLA

H.D. Hunter

The Southern District Publishing Company

Macon, Georgia

Torment

A Novella

H.D. Hunter

© 2018, H.D. Hunter.

Cover Design: Matt Herndon of Custom Graphics Atlanta

Cover Art: Mandela Wise

Interior Formatting: Concierge Self-Publishing

ISBN: 978-0-692-06753-6

For Charli

grass is green.

there's space for grass here.

and,

someone

the same someone has cared enough to water it for years.

time go slow.

time stand still.

time tick tocks backwards.

why does home make me feel like I took a step backwards?

why did time stop?

fly over.

fly through.

rarely, if ever

fly to.

what flies here

won't fly there.

being from nowhere means being unprepared.

Excerpt from *Somewhere* by Gabrielle Hickmon

gabriellehickmon.com | @gabgotti

mothers they like God. they got a special love for all their children, even the rotten ones, even the ones who can't seem to understand her.

by Kierra Wooden

kierrawooden.com

black, skinny, and lanky

Some people make you wanna be something you've never been before. They make you believe you *can* be. That's like Aquila. People in our family used to say she was named after some kind of star or something. Or, another time, they said she was named after an eagle that carried thunderbolts for Zeus. But my sister never carried anybody else's thunderbolts. That's not what she was made for. She was lightning in the sky herself. I guess sometimes people get named wrong.

I remember waiting for her on the porch. Our whole family was in town for the funeral. My aunt Nell said she knew I was waiting on Quila because I was "lookin' at that phone, smilin' like a fool." It had been awhile since I had seen my sister. Even though the occasion was a sad one, I hoped I would have a chance to hear that goofy laugh that gave her away as a small-town girl, no matter how big and successful she got. It was almost like she was waiting for our aunt to go into the house.

No sooner than Aunt Nell had crossed the threshold did Quila pull up in an all-black car with dark window tints. I squinted from the porch like I was trying to see who was inside, but I knew it had to be Quila. Nobody else in our town could afford anything so nice, and if they could, they wouldn't be driving it past my aunt's house.

Quila rolled down the passenger-side window and whisper-yelled up to the porch, "Get in before they see me!"

I was off the porch and into the car in a flash.

It only took us about ten minutes to get to the cemetery from the house. Quila and I sat out in the July sun, not talking for a while. Over the years, we had developed a habit of visiting the graves of close loved ones *before* the burial. During and after was always too busy, crowded. Going early—leaving a little positive energy for when the body came—was almost like leaving a letter waiting in the mailbox.

I twirled a dandelion between my thumb and forefinger, blew all the seeds into the breeze with one puff, and watched them scatter among the headstones and plastic flowers left by the grieving family members of the many dead and gone. All the seeds were together, and just that quickly, they all had new lives, new homes—a new future. They would never be as close as they had once been. They reminded me of us.

"Why didn't you want nobody at the house to see you?"

"It's always much ado about nothing with them," Quila said. "I love 'em, but I wanted a chance to come out here and pay my respects in peace and quiet. Once I go in the house, all the talk will be about cars and jackets, vacations, and all manner of other things that don't matter right now. Don't matter much of anything, no matter the when. Besides … I wanted to say goodbye before they came out here actin' cinematic, too." She chuckled.

"Like Aunt Josie?" I laughed.

"Just like Aunt Josie."

Our aunt Josie had done a triple salchow spin of grief and despair during the viewing before the last family funeral. She plopped right down on the closed part of the casket with my "uncle" Herbert, who was neither her husband nor her brother, in it. One of the legs of the platform holding the casket buckled, and the whole thing tilted downward. The force knocked Aunt Josie off balance, and she toppled over into the half-open casket, right on top of Uncle Herb.

The whole thing caused quite a scene, and the organist, who had anxiety issues, just played faster and faster as my other aunts and uncles tried to pull their sister out. Quila and I sat in the back of the room, snickering the whole time.

"How about you, though? How you been?" Quila

asked me.

I drew an indiscernible pattern in the dirt with a stick I had found.

"Out on your own, now? That's exciting, right? How's it going?" she asked.

I just kept drawing. I'd known what I was making at first, but I wasn't so sure now.

Quila turned away from me and back toward the other graves in the cemetery. She was almost done with her cigarette, and I knew we would go back to Aunt Nell's house when she finished. I admired her while she gazed. It had been plenty long since I'd had the chance. Her skin was a deep brown, almost literally black—the kind of black our people say means you come from royalty.

She was petite, always had been, but she radiated fortitude. Her hair was like straw. She had always hated combing it, ever since she was a child. When Mama took too long to do Quila's hair the night before a big presentation at school, Quila would tell her that having the right words in her presentation at school the next day was more important than having her hair lay down. She had a few more streaks of gray than the last time I'd seen her, but her face was still smooth.

She had a timeless kind of beauty. Soft, brown

eyes, tiny and circular, a perfect match for her button nose. My uncle Roy used to say she was cuter than a workshop elf when she was younger, and then he tried to get her into modeling as she matured. He found himself wanting to be her manager, I reckon. Her lips weren't large, but they were full, and she always wore the perfect lipstick to make them stand out against her skin. Sitting there, smoking, staring off into the distance, she looked like she should be in a movie, or on a poster. But she always looked like that. Picturesque. Thunderbolt Quila, as beautiful as ever.

I walked back to the car and got in. I wanted her to have a last few moments alone to say her goodbye.

* * *

We pulled up to the house around the back way. We thought it would give us more time unnoticed, but not long after we parked, we could see fingers pulling down blinds and eyes peeping through.

Quila sat quiet, not unbuckling her seat belt.

"What's wrong, Quila?"

"I was just thinking. I've gone all these places, done all this work, won all these awards. When we were growing up, all everybody ever said was *make a name for yourself, make a name for yourself.* So, that's what I did. I spent so much time deciding who I wanted to be, then chasing that vision, then achieving it. I should be happy about that, right? But it still feels weird. I don't know ... It still feels weird to come home and feel like I don't know who I am. Or like I'm not who I was. I don't know."

I took her hand in mine. "You're still black, skinny, and lanky to me," I said, "even in all your splendor."

She squeezed my hand gently, glanced at me, and smiled. "That *is* my splendor, boy," she said, then looked down toward her feet, still grinning.

Aunt Josie burst out of the back door and galloped down the steps.

"Lord, hammercy, Aquila! Mmm mmm mmm! It's SO good to see you. *Now*, what kind of great big ole car is this here you got?!"

nowhere

I'm from nowhere. Me, Mama, Quila, our
family—we all from the same place. Nowhere.
Nowhere special, anyway. That's what we say to
people whenever they ask where our people come
from. It's normally easier than trying to describe
the sleepy town, midwestern in location, southern
in spirit.

The town two towns over is one of the mid-size
cities in our state. I reckon that don't amount to
very much, as it were, but it may give you an idea
of how small our place is. A "pass-through" state
is how we call it. Not somewhere that people
come to visit or dream about seeing. Just
somewhere that folks pass through on their way to
somewhere with more to offer. Mama used to say
she figures our folks way back got tired on their
way to somewhere farther and decided to rest a
spell instead of passing through. I reckon they had
a rather long spell, or else they gave up on greener
grass, because here we are.

We been here as far back as Mama knew about.
Her mama, and her mama's daddy, on back and
back even further to people I ain't never heard of.
It's a small place, but Mama used to tell us that
the world is made up of small places.

The big ones don't get so much attention because they're big … they get it because they're rare. Mostly, the world is just small places, with small people; everybody working the best they can, some to get to something bigger, some because it's all they know. I felt powerful coming from a small place when Mama would say that. I felt normal.

Mostly everybody here knows each other. Our families have been so close for so long that we know the patterns. And even though times and people change, the patterns stay the same.

The Wilson family—twins run in the blood over there. The Rogers kin been running a corner store for decades. Ms. Rose, ironically and simultaneously to no one's surprise, use to tend the most beautiful garden in our whole city. If you were going to propose to your sweetheart, you had to do it with a bouquet of Rose's roses or it just wasn't proper.

When she passed (bless her soul), her youngest daughter, Rosalie, took up the garden. There were three girls ahead of her, but Ms. Rose always used to say her baby was the only one who had the touch like she had, the green thumb. Ms. Rose was a youngest too, so she figured it was on account of that. Family lineage runs funny like that sometimes.

On Sundays, we went to church, same as

everybody else. Friday afternoons, kids played in the park downtown. We celebrated births together, mourned together. Our own little community, imperfect but satisfactory. By no stretch of the imagination was it amazing, but it was always home. It always felt like home.

On a clear summer night, the stars would shimmer, and from where we sat it looked like they were a part of our sky and no one else's. You could hear the crickets chirping and see the lightning bugs searching for each other. Time moved slowly there. Kids grew up slow, too. Held hands, shared first dances; first kisses under those same stars.

Parents walked the schoolchildren to the bus and knew the driver by name. There wasn't too much crime to speak of, maybe the occasional lapse in judgment. But even when those situations arose, charges usually weren't filed. Nobody wanted to do anybody harm—at least that's how it seemed, and if everything ended up alright, then everything was alright.

Our town was a black town—still is. Sure, there's some white folks there. Other minorities too, but it's mostly black folks. I reckon there is a "white side of town," but it's so small, not too many people seem to think of it that way. For the most part, the white folks who live in the community been getting along with the rest of us for so long that they just like family too. And if not, your grandma will tell you, "Don't go messin' around with them such and suches; we don't bother them and they don't bother us."

Life lessons don't have to be explicit in our town. We learn a lot by being. By breathing. Almost everything we need to know is in the air. I guess if I had to say anything else about Nowhere, I'd say that, to most of us, it feels like the only place that matters. The town has a strange way of pacifying its citizens. People get here and never want to leave.

Churches would preach that our town was a haven, closest thing to heaven. Schoolteachers, when they *had* to cover geography, would do a rapid survey of the faraway lands, nation states, and bright, colorful oceans. They'd reluctantly teach us about how these places existed, but there was always an undertone of disdain in their voices.

Normally, a lecture would end with some commentary about beautiful things our town had to offer. They'd draw a stark contrast between the hustle and bustle of Tokyo and the quiet peace of Nowhere. Why concern ourselves with the aurora lights of Alaska? Weren't our stars pretty enough without having to endure that cold? At that time, they were. Beautiful enough for mostly all of us.

Other places were pretty as a picture, too. But that's how most folks thought they should remain.

Just pictures. Pictures in our minds and hearts, fun to think about, unnecessary to ever visit.

"That world will chew you up and spit you out," they said. "No matter where you go, you're never going to be treated the way folks around here treat you. Never going to be loved like this town will love you. Never going to be cared for like you will here."

The irony lies heavy on my tongue.

crazy // wildflowers

I think I was in the eighth grade when they told me I was crazy. Quila was in the twelfth. Our younger siblings were too young to know what was going on. I had so many meetings with the guidance counselor about my outbursts in class, she decided it would be best for me to see an outside-of-school counselor. We didn't have money for that. To this day, I'm pretty sure I've never heard any black folks in our community talk about psychological counseling. Mama whooped me a few times for acting out and sent me back to school.

I kept getting in trouble, and, finally, our guidance counselor convinced the principal to let an outside-of-school counselor come to the school to meet me. He was a tall, strong-looking man with a beard that was growing back but not quite grown. He smelled like Old Spice and wore these shiny brown shoes that I couldn't take my eyes off of. Come to think of it, I don't think the school ever asked Mama if it was okay that I talked to the man counselor. But when I told her about it, she wasn't too mad, just told me not to be "tellin' him all our business."

The man asked me a lot of questions. I don't

remember most of them. What I do remember are those shoes. I stared at the man's feet as he talked to me. He asked me about home and my feelings. If I ever got mad or sad ... if I had trouble focusing ... what I liked to think about when I wasn't in school. Sometimes I answered, and other times I just kept staring at those shoes.

They were so shiny. I imagined they were two shiny tortoises, probably tortoise royalty on their island, and that they had been married for hundreds of years. They were greedy and always making the other tortoises bring them leaves and things to eat. Eventually, some men who looked just like the man counselor came to the island and were greeted by the royal tortoises. They asked to see all the other tortoises, and the two royals declined to show them. But after the man counselors offered to bring them lots of leaves and vegetables, they decided to lead them into the village. When they got to the village, the man counselors immediately went to work collecting the village tortoises. They put them in large buckets and dragged the buckets across the sand, back toward their ships.

The royals were scared and realized what a pitiful thing they had done. They begged the man counselors to stop, but nothing could slow them down. Finally, they offered up themselves, being the largest, oldest, and wisest tortoises, to be taken instead of all of their family, friends, and subjects. The men pondered for a moment and considered. They decided to agree to the deal, on one condition: they had been planning to eat the tortoises they collected, but since they would be coming home with two shiny, beautiful, large tortoises, instead of dozens of small, dusty ones, the two royals would become pets for their leader and have to do whatever he asked. The royals agreed immediately, were taken from the island, and never saw their village again.

When they arrived in the land of the man counselors, they were taken to the leader. He was amazed at how shiny and sturdy their shells were. He decided he would like the royals to accompany him everywhere he went. He said that their tough shells would allow him to walk treacherous paths without fear of harm, and the beauty of the shells would attract—

"Do you understand?" the man asked.

"Huh?"

"I'm asking if you understand everything I was just mentioning."

"Yes, sir. I understand," I lied.

"Okay, well, I want you to take this note to your mother. My phone number is on it. Please have her call me as soon as possible."

We were sitting at the dinner table later that night, and I figured it was best to tell Mama about the man counselor then. She told us countless times she "ain't too much like to be bothered" with us after dinner. After dinner was "get ready for bed" time, and I didn't want to upset her then. All of us were around the table, most of my siblings with their heads down, eating like they were starving. In hindsight, they probably were. With four of us, food was often scarce, and even though Mama would tell us not to be in public "actin' like we hungry," she didn't get on us too much for it at home.

Sometimes she would pop Daniel if he was eating with his hands, or call us wild animals for licking our plates clean, but she understood. I don't remember seeing her eat, many of those nights.

She would have a cup of coffee or tea and just watch us. As we got older, Quila started taking after her. She would give almost all of her food to Daniel or Marco before we ever got to the table. Her and Mama would end up watching all of us dive into our plates, sitting side by side, sipping their tea.

Daniel. That's my youngest brother. He was a tiny kid with big eyes that were somehow still beady. His mouth was fifty percent of his face when he was younger, which meant that every time he smiled, he could light up an entire room. He was energetic, caring, and sensitive about stuff most little boys didn't think twice about.

He loved butterflies. One time he brought an orange butterfly into the house. It had taken a liking to him and hung out on his shirt for what seemed like hours. Mama let Daniel do all manner of silly things because he was such a sweet boy. He wasn't very sharp and had to take the special classes at school, but nobody bothered him too much. Whenever we had spaghetti, Daniel had his whole face in his plate, slurping away, only coming up to breathe and giggle.

Marco was born a year before Daniel. He was a quiet boy with curly hair and a cautious gaze. He was very slow to speak most times. He was quiet for so long as a child, Mama thought he might not be able to ever talk, but once he grew up a little bit, we learned that he just liked to think a long time before he said anything. Marco didn't like spaghetti. He didn't like a lot of things, but he wasn't the type to protest. He pretty much just got along however he could.

He didn't talk to me much, but he *loved* Quila. "Key-key," he would call her. Marco would sit at her feet as she did homework, and he always walked her to the door when she went out with her friends. Marco loved to read and would sit for hours on end with his head in a book. His books were some of the only things he would talk about to anybody. I think it was easier for Mama to love Daniel, because he was so kind and cheerful. She sure tried hard with Marco, though.

Marco died that year, when I was in the eighth grade and Quila was in the twelfth. After he was gone, I could really tell that Mama had loved him. She took it harder than anybody, even Quila.

Marco had walked to the bus stop alone one morning. He normally walked with Daniel because they went to the same school, but that day, Mama had to take Daniel to a doctor's appointment. Marco was a responsible kid, and she knew he could walk himself.

But sometime before the bus came, he got hit by a car. Hit and run. We never found out who did it. We buried him on a Saturday. The cemetery he's in has a field of wildflowers. You couldn't make it to his grave without walking through ten thousand of them. They were there, all around his grave marker. Months later, Mr. Po, one of our neighbors who used to give Marco books a lot, drew up this fancy headstone for him and showed it to Mama. It had all the important information about his life and some fancy quote. Mama didn't like it. She said that Marco would have needed to write his own line to have one he appreciated. I wonder how she knew. But I believe that she did know.

Quila didn't used to be too fond of me. We were

opposites. I think Quila had to grow up too fast, playing second parent to three younger siblings. But I always had a deeper connection with Quila. The type of help I couldn't give myself, I could easily give her. She was like that with me, too.

I may be the only person who has ever felt comfortable ... who she has ever *allowed* to challenge her. I would be the one to tell Quila that she wasn't getting enough sleep or eating right. That she didn't have to stress so much about this or that. Pride and authority maybe made her feel threatened that a fourteen-year-old might understand a little bit more about life than an eighteen-year-old. But the truth is, I never understood more about life than Quila. I just saw things in a different way. We didn't figure that out until later, but once we did, our relationship got better.

Quila looked about exactly the same as she does now, but her hair is a little longer. Her smile, though not often seen, was just as bright as Daniel's, but smaller.

She was one of the most popular girls in school, and even though she didn't date, the popular guys would always say that she was pretty for a dark-skinned girl. Her and Mama didn't favor much, but their mannerisms were eerily congruent. They looked most alike on two occasions: when they argued with each other and when they sat at the dinner table, sipping from their cups, watching the rest of us eat.

Pretty much everything else about them was different, though. Mama looked like all of us, or none of us, maybe. We all looked like pieces of her, I reckon. She was the only one of us that was caramel colored, and the only one that was chubby, but she said that's because she had so many babies.

Her hips and legs were thick and toned. She would tell us how she ran track in high school and almost made it to the state meet if it weren't for Dorothy Jensen and the new shoes her parents had bought her. Mama "wore the same shoes all through high school." All Mama's stories had some kind of Dorothy Jensen in them, but she didn't seem too bitter. She would just lean her head back and laugh, covering her teeth with her hand.

Her laugh was like summer rain. Mama had a wide, flat nose and square teeth, and her cheeks were fat and freckled. Her chubby face made her eyes squinty. She had a mass of kinky hair sprouting like a bush from her head, and she usually tied it up with some fancy-colored scarf or bandana. She told us that she used to be slim like Quila. *I used to look just like your sister*, she would say with this far off gaze, almost like she could see the old her.

I still had to give Mama the letter. She was close

to finishing her coffee, so I slipped the crumpled paper from the man counselor out of my pocket and cleared my throat.

"Mama, they gave me this at school. I think I'm in trouble." I slid the note across the table to her.

Everybody kept eating, and Mama grabbed the paper, unfolding it with one hand. She didn't seem too surprised at my comment, probably on account of how I was always getting in trouble, but I waited for a more emotive response. She read the note over the top of her coffee without ever putting her cup down. It took her a long time to read it; longer than I thought it should have, but I don't know, not everybody reads fast.

"What did you tell that man?" Mama finally finished the note.

"Not too much, Mama. Just what we talked about. I wasn't in there tellin' no business. He was just asking me how I feel and what I think about."

"Hmph." Mama furrowed her brow and pursed her lips.

"They sayin' you crazy, boy. They done wrote a list of things in here what's wrong with you. Personality somethin'-or-another … say you got an attention problem, too. They want me to bring you to a man's office so they can do some more tests on you and give you some drugs to take. You wanna go down there? You think that's what you need?"

I didn't know what any of it meant. Mama's questions weren't genuine. She wasn't asking me what I thought I needed; she was asking me if what I thought about the man counselor's note made more sense than what she had told me a thousand times, which was that I needed to "straighten up and act right." In truth, it didn't make more sense.

So I didn't feel bad telling her no.

No sooner had I expressed disinterest in going to the man counselor's office than my mother flung the note back across the table at me, grabbed Daniel's plate, and headed to the kitchen to begin cleaning up. "Good. We ain't got no money for drugs no how," she said, sauntering off.

I looked down and saw words I didn't know, like *neurotic* and *psychosis*. I didn't look them up, though. I lifted my head to Quila staring at me blankly.

Depression would come later in life. I would eventually learn for myself what the man counselor's note had meant and how many psychological issues I had been struggling with, even since childhood. At the time I learned about myself, in adulthood, it seemed that I was probably too damaged to ever make a full recovery, and I ain't never been too keen on taking medicine, so I figured I was doomed.

I learned that I had all these issues after Mama passed away. Not knowing where I could turn made everything else that much harder to deal with. I always knew I was different, but I never figured I was broken. Broken from jump. Like I never had a chance to be normal. I hadn't known. Even if I would have known, what was there to do?

That same night, after dinner and dishes, Quila called me, Daniel, and Marco into her room. She normally didn't like us in there, especially not to sleep. We took up too much space in the bed. Quila had her own room on account of needing girl privacy and because she's the oldest. Usually, I shared a room with Marco and Daniel, who slept on bunk beds. I never liked beds too much, and Mama bought me a comfy sleeping bag and extra pillows, and so it worked out that the apartment we lived in only had two rooms.

Mama slept downstairs in the living room on the couch bed that folded out. Every so often, Quila would try to get Mama to live in her room so she could live downstairs, but Mama always said she preferred to be in the living room. Mama kept a pistol down there, and wanted to always keep watch on the door, especially during the night time when break-ins happened more frequently in our neighborhood.

We all filed into Quila's room with our pajamas on and got in the bed. She had a lamp on and gave us all a hug and a kiss on the forehead before we laid down. Her eyes were red and watery. I wanted to ask her why she had been crying, but something told me it wasn't a good time.

Even after we turned out the lights, I could hear her sniffling and holding back groans. I imagined the tears rolling down her face in the dark, her wiping them on the pillowcase before she had to believe they were real.

Once, before I fell asleep, I reached out and touched her foot while she was sniffling. The room went silent, and after a couple moments, I felt the tension go out of her leg. I figure she went to sleep after that, because I didn't hear too much more out of her. I reckon I went to sleep pretty soon after that myself.

Quila had a full-size bed. She slept on the left side, next to the alarm clock. Daniel slept on the right. I laid horizontally across the foot of the bed, trying to avoid Quila's feet. Marco slept in the middle, and we laid all around him, like wildflowers.

"The Talented Tenth"

After Quila learned I was "special," she became a better big sister. She was much kinder to me, and sometimes, she'd even come by the school and walk home with me, buying ice cream for us to eat on the way. I figured she was taking pity on me, and I didn't want her to be sweet just because I was special. I didn't *feel* special. I just felt like me. But it was nice having a real big sister for a change, so I didn't make a fuss.

They ended up moving me to what the kids called the "slow class." One version of the slow class had kids with physical disabilities who needed assistance to make it through the day. The other version was filled with kids who might look close to normal at first glance but who were "special" in their own way. I was in the second version.

There were about seven of us in there with two teachers. Some of the kids couldn't speak. Some of them just couldn't think right. I didn't need as much help as them, so I pretty much kept to myself most of the time and did all the easy work they gave me.

Sometimes, Ms. Margaret, one of our teachers, would go to the real class and get assignments from them and give them to me. She would also bring me extra books from the school library to read while they attended to the other students. Students were only allowed to check out two books at a time, but teachers could get as many as they wanted.

I think she knew I wasn't supposed to be in that kind of slow class, but I reckon there wasn't another kind of slow class to put me in. I guess she pitied me too, but my mind was changing about pity: it wasn't so bad when people chose to do nice things for me. I'd do the extra assignments and then try to help with the other kids in class. My teachers told me it wouldn't be quite the same when I got to the high school. They said it'd be better. The school year was almost over anyway.

One day I went to watch one of Quila's last softball games of the season. She was a star on the team, and it was her senior season. Not many of the girls liked her on account of she was so good, but the same reason they hated her was the same reason they loved her when they won games.

The sun wouldn't let my eyes open more than halfway. Not a cloud in the sky. Some of the girls on the team whose parents had a little money had these fancy sunshades on. But Quila and the rest of the kids like us on the team just pulled the brims of their hats down real low and wiped the sweat out of their eyes with their wristbands.

Quila was having a pretty good game, and her team was winning by a bunch, so it wasn't fun to be out there. I picked at weeds in the grass by the bleachers most of the game, especially the times Quila's team was on defense; it was boring. In one of the last innings, Quila made an error. It rarely happened, so a lot of people in the crowd gasped and murmured when they saw it. I'm not sure if it was a mindless moment or if Quila just didn't care, but I'd never seen her do anything like it before.

There was a batter up, runners on first and third. Quila was playing third base. The girl at bat hit a pop fly right over Quila's head; she backpedaled and jumped high into the air, stretching out her glove. Her black arm glistened in the sun, like a branch against the blue sky. It really was a wonderful catch. She came down with the ball, took one step and threw a rocket to second base.

The rocket was too high though. Quila threw the ball right over her teammate's head. The girl who had been on third crossed home plate easily. The runner rounding second made it to third by the time Quila's teammates retrieved her errant ball. The scoreboard went up one point for the visiting team, and the girls in the visiting dugout cheered and jeered. The next runner at bat hit a similar pop fly between second and third, and Quila's shortstop, a girl named Steph, caught it easily. Both teams headed to their dugouts to swap offense for defense.

The bleachers near me were also close to the dugout, so I saw everything that happened next. Joanie Sparks was one of the only white girls in our whole school and a captain on the softball team. Nobody could too much figure out why Joanie, with parents with all that money, would be going to our school. Mama used to say her daddy "probably may run for office in the next couple years, and he's gonna need that black vote." She figured if he and his family tried to get in extra good with the black folks in our town, then black folks would probably be more willing to vote for him.

Well, Joanie was pretty mad that Quila let that girl score. It ain't seem like such a big deal, because they were winning by so much, but I guess when you're mad, you're just mad. For some reason, Joanie gave Quila an earful about not wanting that team to score and rack up tallies. A big earful. At first, Quila tried to be civil, even apologetic. But Joanie just kept asking why. *Why? Why? Why'd you do that, Aquila? Why'd you make that stupid play? Why'd you let them score again? Don't you have nothing to say?*

Quila sat in the dugout and tried to ignore Joanie, but she just kept on going. I didn't listen to the whole thing. After a while it got annoying. But the last thing I heard, and the thing that made Quila jump up, was this:

27

"Nothing, huh? Well, that's just great, Aquila. You make the dumbest play of the game and don't even have nothing to say for yourself. All your little brothers either slow or just plain stupid, so I figure it was only a matter of time until we realized you ain't no different."

Even from where I was standing, I saw Quila's whole body get stiff. She scrambled up to her feet and started toward Joanie with her fists balled up. Joanie, somehow surprised at how angry Quila was, backed up against the metal cage in the dugout and put her hands up to cover herself. Quila cocked her fist back, but she didn't swing. As she stood there looking at Joanie, she started to cry. Quila threw off her hat and climbed out of the dugout. She was speedwalking toward my bleacher. She brushed past me and muttered, "Come on." That's when I saw Joanie Sparks running out of the dugout toward us.

Now, I don't too much remember what I was thinking. I didn't feel like Joanie could whoop Quila. I mean, she was sneaking up on her, and sometimes that gives a person an advantage. I wasn't worried though. It almost halfway looked like Joanie was running up to apologize. But she was moving pretty fast, and I don't know, maybe I just got scared. Right as she was passing me, and maybe fifteen feet from Quila, I stuck my leg out real quick-like and tripped her. Joanie Sparks fell face flat in all them weeds I had been picking at for the whole game. Her cheek landed right next to a tiny anthill.

Quila turned around when she heard the thud. Some of the other girls on the team back in the dugout cackled. Joanie got up, face as red as all get out. She had smudges of dirt on her cheek and fire in her eyes. I was stuttering and nervous. I thought she might hit me, and I know I'm not supposed to hit a girl, so I didn't know what to do. Quila came back near us while Joanie was huffing and puffing, laughing hysterically.

"Don't be mad at him, Joanie. He's *special*."

Quila kept laughing as we turned to walk home. She was in such good spirits the whole way. We even stopped and got some ice cream. That was normally only an afterschool thing. Quila's team went to the playoffs that year to try to make a run for the state championship. There were only a few more games in the season after that one, but she didn't go back. She stopped playing after that game.

Sometimes I'd walk by her room and see her with her cleats on, twirling her bat around and around, making fun like she was up at bat and swinging away in slow motion.

She'd take the cleats off and put them up against the wall, lean the bat up against the wall right next to them. She never put them away, but I never saw her take them back to the softball field again. I'd get sad when I saw that bat and those cleats just sitting there like that.

One night I knocked on Quila's door while she was twirling her bat. She took her cleats off, propped the bat up, and told me to come in.

"Quila, I wanted to ask you about something I learned in school today."

"What's up?"

"Ms. Margaret brought me this book back from the library, and I was reading, but some of it I don't understand."

Quila ran her hands over the cover and opened it up to a random page in the middle. It was a middle-school version of a biography of W.E.B. Dubois.

"This is a good one," she said.

"I don't get the talented ten part, Quila."

"The Talented *Tenth*. What's not to get?"

"Well ... who are they? Seem like ten people shouldn't be that hard to list."

Quila chuckled and handed me the book back. "Say there are a hundred black people in the world. You, me, the little guys, Mama—"

"Derrick?" I blurted. Derrick was my friend from school.

"Mmm hmm, Derrick too. Anyway, there's all of us, and then more people to make up a hundred. Well, what W.E.B. Dubois thought is that that ninety of us would be regular. That's a lot, right? Just regular folks who do regular things. Maybe truck drivers or work in stores or something. But ten of us, and it don't matter which ten, would be brilliant. Super smart and super strong, kinda like superheroes. He felt like no matter what, those ten people would be responsible for helping the other ninety, because they knew more and could do more."

"He was one of the ten, huh?" I asked, after considering for a moment.

"I'm sure he thought of himself that way." Quila nodded.

I sat quiet for a minute, taking it all in.

"Something bothering you, champ?" Quila asked.

"I'm in the ninety, ain't I, Quila?"

She looked at me sideways, then down at the carpet. She started tapping her feet the way she do when she's trying to think of a good way to say something.

31

"Lot of people would say you're in the ninety. But you're in the ten to me."

"Because I'm special."

"Being special ain't real. It's just something people made up for when they don't understand somebody. I mean, there are kids that need help, I know that. Some people wasn't born with everything they was supposed to be born with. But people like to call you special when they don't know what else to call you. You ain't never been *special* to me. Just different."

I was quiet.

"I see the way you read them books, faster than all the other kids, even faster than me and Mama sometimes. And you learn as quick as anybody's business. I think if nobody ever told you there was anything wrong with you, you'd be going along doing fine, just like anybody else. Maybe even better."

I picked up the book and slouched out of the room. Right before I was through the door, I turned around.

"Hey, Quila …"

"Yes?"

"What's it like to be in the ten?"

Quila started tapping her foot again.

"It's not all it's cracked up to be, honey." Her face was puzzled. She stared down at the carpet, still tapping her feet, her mind somewhere much further away than that bedroom. "It's not all it's cracked up to be, at all."

scars that don't heal

Quila and I made it into Aunt Nell's house and settled in. My aunts had teamed up to cook a big meal for the family members arriving in town that day, which was most of them. Aunt Nell, Aunt Josie, Uncle Don, and the rest of the family sat around in a circle, eyes locked on Quila. It was like this every blue moon that she was around.

"So, you make commercials?" Uncle Don asked. "What do you do?"

"Kind of, Unc. I have people that work for me … like creative people. They come up with most of the ideas for other companies that need our help. It's called consulting."

"Hmm, so what you do is have *your people* make commercials for other people?" Aunt Nell this time.

Quila chuckled. "Well, it's more than just commercials, but yes, Auntie. If somebody wants to do some marketing, we're a solid partner. A lot of commercials and other advertisements reach people through digital and social media these days—websites and Facebook, you know? So, it's not always putting stuff on TV like it used to be."

"And you say it's all black people up there, huh?" asked Aunt Josie. "I didn't know black folks had these kinds of companies."

"Black people got everything white folks got, Auntie. That side of the story just isn't always told. Yeah, the company is mostly black employees. From all over the world, though. Black people from Ghana, Jamaica, Brazil. We're always learning something new about the world. There are some Latino folks too. It's a good mix. But we specialize in helping companies—making commercials for companies—who are owned by minorities, or if their primary customers are minorities. We work with a lot of 501(c)(3) companies—charities."

"That takes a certain level of cultural sensitivity, right, Quila? To combine so many people in one company who are able to understand other groups, what they want and need to hear, and how to reach them? You must have some amazing people that work for you. That's not a small thing," I chimed in.

I loved egging Quila on. She's a philosopher, and even though she doesn't like to brag, she can't avoid a good conversation about race or ethnicity or sexuality or anything else in the world that folks know is important but act too scared to speak on.

Quila took a sip of her drink before responding.

"Super talented people who work with me, and yes, very culturally aware. You know, all these years we've been looking to white businesses, white business owners, white modes of operation as our standard. But it's a new day."

I snuck glances at our relatives as Quila continued her monologue. Some were leaned in across the table, eyes locked in on Quila. Uncle Don picked at his fingernails. Aunt Josie nodded and nudged Aunt Nell, who was sitting next to her, after every few words Quila said, a dead giveaway that she didn't understand too much of what Quila was talking about.

"I think people are realizing that our ideas and what we have to offer are just as valuable, if not more relevant, to our communities than these other organizations that come in just trying to play the role to make the sale. My company donates millions of dollars to local and national charities every year. We help put little black boys and girls through college, send them to camp for the summer. We make a lot of money, but nobody seems greedy, you know?"

Everybody nodded, with murmurs of agreement.

"I go to work with a clean conscience every day, because even though it's *business*, even though we're making a lot of money, I don't feel like we're exploiting the community. There's always more we can do, you know? But I'm proud of us."

"So, Quila. What do you *do*?" I asked.

Quila smiled. "I help black people in any way I can to be more empowered, more inspired, and more successful."

"Damn, they pay folks to do that?!" called out Uncle Curtis. Uncle Curtis never passed up the opportunity to get a good exclamatory joke in edgewise. Everybody laughed accordingly. Politely.

Most of the family sat around, staring at Quila with their eyes wide. How many of these concepts had they had ever considered? But that's why I appreciated it when Quila came back. She had a way of speaking that was able to expand people's minds. It could be anybody else saying the same thing and it just wouldn't seem true ... wouldn't seem real. But Quila was the real deal. I never wanted her to stay long, on account of *somebody* had to leave this place and be amazing. But I always figured if she could spend a long time back here and not be negatively affected by it, she could change the whole town.

But then I'd get to thinking about if there was any real value in changing this town, or if it would be better if we all just packed up and left it how it is, started over. I never got to a good answer, no matter how long I thought. Maybe that's why people stay here so long. Get stuck here, playing mental tennis between "Go" and "Stay." By the time they look up, the sun is dimming on their days, and it's time to lay down. It's more sad than beautiful.

Quila and I stayed up washing dishes while the rest of the family got ready for bed. The funeral was in the morning, and even after it was over, there would be a long day, what with the repast, then gathering back at the house and whatnot. Most people weren't returning home until the day after the funeral anyway. I was scrubbing a stubborn speck of spaghetti sauce from a pot, my face leaned in so close I had dish soap on my nose. It just wouldn't go away. Quila gently grabbed my shoulder.

"Let me get that."

Quila took the pot from me and scrubbed the speck away with a flick of her wrist. We kept washing dishes in silence for a little while. I could tell Quila wanted to say something.

"How are you? You didn't answer me back at the cemetery. I know it can't be easy bei—" she began.

"You remember that time we were riding our bikes down that big hill?"

She paused for a moment. "Yeah. Over by Rosary Square."

"Mmm hmm. Remember when you flipped your bike over? Skinned your legs all up? Down to the white meat, and you was crying?"

"It hurt!"

"Remember you was crying so bad you wouldn't let nobody touch you or put no peroxide on you or nothing? And Mama kept telling you it was gonna be okay, but you just kept crying."

"Yeah …?"

"You remember what happened after?"

"I think so. Mama took me to the doctor. Only I don't think he was a real doctor. But either way, he worked in the pharmacy downstairs from our apartment, so it seemed real enough to me at the time. He calmed me down some and gave me a sucker. He rubbed stuff on my legs and patched me all up, and we went home."

"That's it?"

"That's all I remember."

I kept scrubbing the dishes. Working on the last pot.

"Hey … I'm just trying to help, okay? I know I haven't been around, but—"

"Do you remember the scars?" I asked.

Quila squinted at me and titled her head to the right, searching.

"We called him Dr. Brown. Dr. Willie Brown, he ran the pharmacy back then. Once you got the sucker you calmed down, but before he put the bandages on you he told you that your scars wasn't gonna heal. Said they would cover up some and look like dark spots, but they wouldn't ever go away. You didn't too much mind, but Mama had a fit about you wearing dresses when you got older. Talkin' about going to prom and getting married and all that other stuff. Yeah … Dr. Brown said you'd be fine, but your legs would never quite look the same."

"Okay. So?"

"You asked me how I am, how I'm doing. It's kinda like that."

"Lotta stuff from the past reminds you of how sad it used to be?"

"There ain't really no used to be. It's like I still got the scars, but they still hurt, too."

Quila finished drying the last pot and put a kettle on to make us some tea. The light was dim in the kitchen. Everybody else had gone on to bed. Everything in the house was old. It had all been the same for as long as I could remember. The cabinets were oak and the countertops gray resin.

The kitchen floor was tiled with flowers that didn't look real, but they sure were pretty.

One small window above the sink would have let in the sun if it were daytime, but the moon crept through just enough to be remembered. The kettle started squealing, and Quila poured us two mugs of lemon tea. I cupped my hands around my mug for warmth, letting the steam climb up my nostrils with my face close to the rim. Quila glanced at me in between quiet sips. My turn to talk.

"You know, we spend all this time looking forward. Go through tough times, and people say it's a process. I'm not sure how much I believe in that anymore, though. What if the pain *was* the process, and everything is different now? Maybe things just change that quick and everything is different forever.

"I spend so much time looking forward, waiting on something better to come, and it ain't coming. Maybe it ain't ever coming. And I can deal with that. But I don't like playing no fool, sitting at the station, thinking every howl of the wind is my train. I'd rather just know." I felt the familiar lump in the back of my throat and burning sensation behind my eyes.

"You been feelin' like this since you moved out on your own, or since before? You know, it was a big thing for you to move out. You've accomplished a lot, but that was spec—that was a

41

major step." Aquila was tender.

"Been feelin' like this a long time, Quila. I don't really care too much what I did. It's what I don't think I can do anymore that bothers me. I been giving it all I got. Piecing together a whole bunch of nothings into what I thought was a something. But I stepped back, looked—I mean really looked. I just got a pile of nothings. And I'm *tired. So tired.*"

My voice cracked and tears ran down my cheeks. Quila walked toward me with her arms outstretched, and I shuffled backward and turned my body away from her. My sobs grew louder. I tried to stifle them on account of everybody sleeping, but the more I tried to hold them in, the louder they got.

Quila cradled my head and neck into her shoulder. She rubbed the back of my head like Mama used to do when I was a little boy. I cried even louder. My arms hung limp at my sides. I was so ashamed. Quila hadn't even been back one night and I had already broken down. I cried because I was sad. Then I got angry because I was crying. Then I cried because I was angry. The more I cried, the uglier it got. Coughs, sobs, stutters—I could feel my whole body shaking as I tried to speak in between sniffles.

"I'm b-broken, Q-Quila. I was made broken."

Quila rubbed my head and squeezed me tight with her left arm.

"Honey," she said. "You're a mosaic."

***

The funeral was peaceful, just how Daniel would have wanted. The sky was a crisp blue with marshmallow clouds. The clouds moved fast that day. Almost seemed like you could watch them rushing across the sky. Rushing to meet my brother.

I read a book once that said when we die, our souls just jump from cloud to cloud throughout eternity, seeing the world, cruising the skies. I think Daniel would like that. He'd have fun. If anybody deserves to see the world and be amazed at every single detail this universe has to offer, it's him.

When the preacher released the doves, they flew so high, it seemed like they got swallowed up by the clouds. Nobody cried too much; I think the thought of Daniel was so strong that it made people happy, no matter what was going on. I sat in the back for the majority of the time. Quila got up toward the end and said some words and thanked people for coming. We both stood up front near the casket after the ceremony to shake hands and hug and cry with the people that had come. I knew I was going to miss my brother. He was only nineteen.

I had a couple of white roses that I tossed into the grave before we all left the cemetery. We had used the last of the money from when Mama died to bury Daniel and have services for him. Everybody said it was a nice service.

The funeral reminded me that I was scared to die. I wasn't scared not to live anymore; living was hard enough. But looking around at everything we did for Daniel, thinking about how much it had cost, I felt trapped. I had come into the world with no money, and now, I couldn't even die without worrying about somebody having to foot the bill for me.

Trapped in life. My therapist at the time said she wanted to meet with me weekly on account of I was a self-harm risk. But as much as I thought about how much easier not living was than living, the money always scared me more. What would people think of me? I would visualize myself handing over the money for Daniel's casket. I would be embarrassed if Quila had to do that for me, but there was nobody else I would rather have do it. Death felt like rain. Life felt like running between the drops.

"Aquila, honey, this was such a nice service, so beautiful. I'm so sorry about Danny Boy. I'm praying for y'all," said Aunt Nell.

"Thanks, Auntie."

"What y'all gon' have at the repast?" Uncle Don asked.

"Same stuff as always, Uncle Don," I chimed in.

"So, some more of that chicken and them greens, huh? Come on, Josie, let's get over there before the Gordon side of the family … you know how they do."

"Oh, Donnell, hush!" Aunt Josie rolled her eyes.

She came over to Quila and me and put her arms around both of us, kissing each of us on the cheek. She squeezed us for a moment too long—the kind of squeeze that's a substitute for words you don't have.

"I love you two."

"We love you too, Auntie," Quila and I said at the same time.

Aunt Josie and Uncle Don turned to go, and Quila and I started toward her car.

"You ready for the *repast*?" Quila asked with facetiously false energy. The post-funeral activities were always her least favorite.

"I feel kinda sick," I said.

Two orange butterflies swirled outside the car window while we sat at a stoplight. The day was bright and beautiful—I was upset that we had to go spend the rest of it inside. We were going to eat in the great hall of the old church downtown, the same church Mama used to take us to when we were little. The space was way too big. Not that many people had come to Daniel's funeral, but the church let us rent it for free, and so we made do. We pushed a few tables together in the middle of the hall, and everybody sat around, quietly eating, until one of our neighbors broke the silence.

"Things sure gonna be different for y'all without Daniel, now, huh?"

making ends meet

When I was about ten years old, I started stealing.
I used to love to watch cops and robbers shows on
the television, and even though the criminals
always got caught, it seemed like fun to have all
those folks chasing you, trying to get what you
got. I reckon I just liked the idea of having all the
attention. I wanted to be chased.

At first it was small stuff: bubble gum, nickels
from the tip bucket at the corner store. The more I
took, though, the more I wanted to take. I didn't
hardly care about the stuff after it was stolen, but
nobody was chasing me over gum and nickels. I
had to take something that was worth running
after. That's when I started stealing groceries.
Mostly everybody in our town was poor and
hungry; at least they would make like they were
whenever they had the chance. I knew food would
be something worth coming after.

The first food I ever stole was a ham, one of those
big ones that Mama would slice and give all of us
pieces. I knew they cost a lot because we would
only eat them if Mr. Po paid for it or if Mama had
extra money from working on the holidays.

It wasn't hard to steal the ham; I just grabbed it

and walked out of the store while the shop owner wasn't paying attention. I walked all the way home, cradling the ham like a newborn, looking over my shoulder for the shop owner or the police or anybody who would want to bring me to justice. About halfway to the house, though, I realized that nobody was coming. I sulked the rest of the way, thinking about what other, more expensive, things I could steal next.

I should have thrown the ham away, but I didn't. I set it on the couch as I came in the house, and I went up to our room. More than anything, I was discouraged at the way the day had gone. I didn't want to talk to anyone. I got into Marco's bed without showering or changing into my pajamas, which Mama always said was a no-no. He and Daniel were at Aunt Josie's for the week. I quickly fell asleep.

I had a dream that night. I was me, but a tree. I could see and feel and hear just like normal, but I was in the shape of a tree. I couldn't move on my own. The wind started to blow, and I swayed from side to side. I wanted to stay still, but there was no way to control myself. The wind blew harder, and I grew tired. Fatigue relaxed me, and the breeze carried me side to side. I let it control me, the wind's rhythm rocking me into a daze, to and fro, to and fro.

Then the thunder came. It boomed through the night, and the rain came down harder. The wind howled and shook me, to and fro, to and fro, even faster than before. I let my tree body move with the wind, but it hurt this time. I shook so hard that fruit started falling from my branches. First just a few, what looked like peaches, then tens, then hundreds … the sound of my fruit falling against the ground was almost as loud as the thunder.

"Wake up, boy! You talkin' in your sleep."

Mama had me by the shoulders, shaking me back and forth so hard my head was rocking. I blinked a bunch of times real fast and opened my eyes wide so she could see I was paying attention.

"Boy, where that ham downstairs come from?"

"It came from the corner store."

Mama pinched my nose real good, like she always did when I told a lie.

"OUCH! Mama, why you pinch me for? I ain't lie!"

"Don't say 'lie,' boy. That's a bad word. I believe you. But I also know you ain't got no money for no ham like this, so *who* got it from the corner store is what I want to know. How did you get this ham?"

I pondered for a second, hoping she couldn't see my nervous expression in the dark. The prospect of another nose pinch seemed awful, so I told the truth … kinda.

"I took it, Mama. I was hungry, and I figured Daniel and y'all was hungry too. So I just sneaked it from the store. I knew it was wrong, but I was too scared to turn back. I'm sorry."

Mama sat on the edge of the bed and cupped her face in her hands. She used to say it was her "I love you, but you working my nerves" position. She let out a sigh.

"It's not good to steal. You know that. People in this town don't have too much, just like us. They work hard for everything they got, just to make ends meet, and we ain't nobody special to take it from 'em. Even if we was, that's just not the kind of people we are.

"I don't want you stealing. We have always made do one way or another, and even though I wish I could do better by y'all, we got pride in our name. Nobody can look down on us and say we needy or beg or steal for nothing, you understand? What would your brothers think, you supposin' to be a role model for them?"

I dropped my head in shame.

"I know you was tryin' to do right. This can be just between us. But please, no more stealing, okay?"

"Okay, Mama."

***

The next week was pretty uneventful. We had ham and eggs that very next morning. Ham and potatoes that night, and so on and so forth. The week after next, though, I stole again.

I needed something bigger this time—something that was going to get more attention. Something that even if people didn't see me take it, they would miss it and try to do some sort of investigation after I was gone.

I thought about the jewelry store, but I didn't know how to get through the glass case. I didn't want to risk going back to the corner store and getting in trouble for the ham, so I steered clear of there. Eventually, though, I thought of the perfect plan.

The diner.

The diner was the coolest spot in town to hang. All of the old church people, high schoolers, and working moms could be found there, depending on the time of day. The diner was always busy, which meant that they were making money. They kept a tip jar at the front register. I guess they figured it was fairer for everybody to split the tips, even if some people worked harder than others. I would steal the tip jar. That way, not just a manager would be trying to catch me, but maybe some people that worked there too! I didn't want to keep the money, but they wouldn't know that. I would take the jar and run, and they'd have to try to catch me.

***

It was a hot night with a cool breeze. The humidity was something you had to get used to where we lived, and we did, but every now and again you'd stop just to breathe or soak up some sunlight, and realize how thick the air was.

Walking was to swimming as breathing was to drowning. There were only two clouds in the sky, drifting slowly but close to each other. In their own world.

I watched my feet for each step I took toward the diner. Focusing on my steps helped me ignore the knot in my throat. The repetitive sound of my footfalls on the sidewalk made me calm. I counted my steps.

One ... two ... three ... Would I be fast enough? Should I take the jar while they watched me, or should I try to sneak and do it? What would the people there think of me? *Forty-four, forty-five, forty-six ...* all of these thoughts scared me, but the excitement of each question gave me the courage I needed to keep walking forward. *One hundred ten, one hundred eleven, one hu*—I was there. My last one hundred twelve steps had brought me to the diner.

It was one of those big diners from the '50s that had been renovated on the inside to keep it looking like the '50s, but operating in the current day. I didn't know what it was called. I'm not sure anybody did. Maybe it didn't have a name. There was a massive lighted sign outside that you could see from a mile away that said "Diner." Around town, it was known as just that. I walked into a space with green-and-white checkered tile, waitresses in aprons, and the smell of grease and sugar.

The light was so bright in the diner, I had to squint as I entered. Everybody was busy, hustling and bustling back and forth. Small and not needing immediate service, I went seemingly unnoticed. It was working-mom time. All the ladies from town in their nurse scrubs, grocery store uniforms, and other job clothes filled the tables, talking and laughing, smoking cigarettes with their coffee, enjoying what was likely their only real free time each day.

A waitress walked by and stepped on my foot.

"Oh, I'm sorry! Watch out, little man."

"I'm sorry," I said.

The knot in my throat returned, and my stomach

started to twist and flip. I could leave and go home, and nothing bad would happen. But I had come so far. I had to do it. I told myself I would, and so I had to. I spied the tip jar on the counter right next to the cash register and made my way over.

My face didn't reach the top of the counter, but I could still see the jar once I got right up close to the stand. A waitress with greasy hair was arguing with a man with a greasy shirt. He looked like the manager. I didn't too much know what a manager looked like, but he was one of the only men I saw in the diner then, so I figured that's what he had to be.

The woman stormed off back toward the grill, snatching her apron off the counter along the way. The man had taken some money out of the cash register and was counting it with his back to the counter. I stood on my tippy toes and swiped the glass jar. I held it low, right by my stomach with two hands. It was heavy, heavier than the ham. I turned and walked out of diner into the humid night air.

I was supposed to be walking slowly, so I could be caught, but my heart was pounding so fast, I was halfway down the street before I realized I was nearly galloping. I slowed down to a trot and eventually stopped altogether to breathe. I held the jar up under the streetlight and examined it. It was a humongous Mason jar with a square of

notebook paper taped to it. It said *TIPS* in a
scribbly font that was highlighted in orange.

The jar was filled about three-quarters of the way
with coins, and a handful of dollars sat on the top.
It wasn't much money, but I thought somebody
would miss it.

Somebody did.

She was like a blur in the night. I didn't know
what I was looking at until it was almost too late.
In a stark white smock and pink apron flapping in
the wind, she was running toward me. I looked
down at the jar in my hands and back at her as she
approached like a raging bull. I turned to run and
stumbled over my feet. I recovered and dashed
off, still gripping the jar—scared and exhilarated
at the same time.

I didn't make it very far, twenty yards at most,
before the waitress caught me. She turned me
around and jacked me up by my shirt collar. I
recognized her as the waitress who had been
arguing with the probably-manager back at the
diner. Her nametag read *Betty*.

"You thought nobody would see your grubby
little hands sneaking off with our tips, huh? We
work hard for them tips!" Betty barked at me.

I had an inappropriately gleeful smile on my face
as she jerked me around by my collar. Betty

whipped her head back and scrunched her face up in disgust. I was just so happy. This is what I had waited for.

"Well? You gonna say something for yourself or just sit there lookin' creepy? I ought to take you back to the diner and make you wipe every table!"

"I'm sorry, ma'am."

"Oh, you'll be sorry!"

Betty snatched the jar from me while keeping a grip on my collar with her off hand. Coins flew out of the top of the jar and splattered into the road, sparkling in the streetlight. She was a strong lady. And fast too. She probably ran track in high school. She didn't look too much older than Quila.

"Matter fact, I think you need to—"

"*Unhand my child.*"

I knew that voice anywhere. I was only one person's child to claim, too.

I turned my neck and Betty looked up to see my mama approaching from across the street. Betty let my collar go and stepped back half a step, planting her feet squarely on the pavement.

Mama walked up, still silent. She wasn't one to

make a big scene. She had always been a very observant person. The girls in her house growing up were encouraged to listen first and speak when necessary, and it had made her perception elite. She looked at me and my collar, Betty and her apron, the tip jar in her hands, the pennies on the asphalt. Then she asked a question she already knew the answer to.

"What is going on here?"

"This child of yours was down at the diner a little earlier. Saw fit to grab our jar of tips we work hard all night for. Walked smooth out the front door. I saw him, ran after him. Told him I would take him back to make him clean tables, but I see he's spoken for now. I was just upset. We got the jar back; I suppose everything is fine," Betty explained.

Mama looked down at me.

"Is this true?"

I nodded and looked at my shoes. I was halfway ready for a slap on the neck, but it never came. When I looked back up, something strange was happening.

Mama had begun to tear up. I had only seen my mama cry a few times, and never when one of us got in trouble. We were usually the ones to cry. But there it was, plain as day, tears sliding down her face. She spoke with a broken voice. There was a hue of sadness in her tone that made my heart feel heavy and slow-beating.

"There's five of us. We do all we can, and we usually don't have no problem. But he just recently started this here; this isn't something we do. He's *special,* you see. He probably heard me saying something about money around the house and thought it was his responsibility to do something. I think it's just a misunderstanding. I'm so sorry. Please don't tell the manager."

Bewildered, I looked at Betty. The menacing visage had softened into a compassionate gaze. She stepped forward to my mama and hugged her. Mama began to sob and Betty rubbed her back. They stood there like that in the street for a while. I stood there confused. Mama and Betty exchanged some words in low tones between sniffles. Betty had started crying too.

"Here, take it."

"I can't do that," Mama said.

"No, I'm serious. We make enough tips in a night; this jar won't hurt us too bad. Besides, the night is just starting; we got plenty more money to make. And nobody saw who took the jar but me, so either one of y'all can come back in there without anybody disturbing you or lookin' at you crazy."

Mama stood there looking like she wanted to cry all over again. Betty reached out and grabbed Mama's hand, turned the palm upright, and put the jar into it.

"You come down whenever you get off one of these nights and I'll fix something up right for you. MacArthur don't too much pay attention unless it benefits him. Me and the girls will make sure you're taken care of."

Mama sobbed again and gave Betty a hug. Then, just like that, the waitress was gone. Mama and I turned to go home. We walked most of the way in silence, but I just had to know.

"Mama, what happened back there?"

"Something only mamas can understand."

"Am I *special*, Mama?"

"You ain't no different from anybody else in any way that counts, boy."

"But you told Betty—"

"*Ms. Betty* to you, little boy. And stop asking me so many questions. I told you I didn't want you stealing no more. I'll deal with you when I get home."

When Mama said there were no more questions,

there were no more questions. I don't remember what my punishment was, but I do remember Mama putting a new coat for Daniel on layaway with the tip money.

I didn't understand at that time ... well, maybe I won't ever understand ... the ties that bind black women and mothers in our world. Our great big world but also the tiny world of our community. All they had was each other.

I did learn something about being *special* that day, though. Funny thing about special is that it sounds like a good thing, but it's not. At least not always. And depending on if somebody means good special or bad special, you'll be treated different. I spent the rest of my life trying to figure out which special to be and when, and how I can be special enough to keep tip jars when I need to. I reckon it's a shame that, for all that figuring, I'm still not sure which kind of special I actually am. I don't know if this thing, this label ... what makes me, *me* ... is good or bad. If *I'm* good or bad. I never craved the pity. I only wanted attention.

our little forever

"Well, what do you mean, *different*?" Aunt Josie responded to our neighbor, confused. "Of course things will be different; the poor baby boy is dead."

"I meant no disrespect, Josie. I just been thinking 'bout how Daniel was a *child of the village*, so to speak. Things will be different for all of us now that he's gone. But, of course, he was closest to y'all. He lived with his brother. I'm just thinking of how different things will be for y'all. I'm sorry. Maybe I'm just talkin' too much now."

"Talking too much and about nothing you know about! Daniel ain't been living with his brother for some time now. I don't know what you gettin' at with these sneaky questions, but you startin' on my nerves!" Aunt Josie snapped back. She had a particular knack for being nosy but hated when other people did it. Ironically, she also had a knack for being messy and oversharing while she was warding off other eavesdroppers and nose-pokers.

Nobody knew that I had moved out on my own except the family. In truth, it wasn't anybody else's business. It probably wasn't theirs.

If I hadn't needed help from Aunt Josie to make arrangements for Daniel after I moved, I'm sure I wouldn't have bothered to tell her and the rest of my aunts and uncles either. Our tiny community sometimes had blurry boundaries. Folks didn't always understand that your life was your life and their life, theirs. Mama used to say, "Small places thrive on small talk." I guess that's all there was to it. But still, I'd had enough of people small-talking about me. It made me feel little.

"What do you mean, not living with his brother? Where else could he live? Aquila, did you know about this?" our neighbor asked.

Nobody was eating anymore. Our nosy neighbor had completely destroyed the mood. Here was our town's infamous gossip, starting before Daniel was even in the ground good.

"I knew what I needed to know," Aquila said quietly yet sternly. Our neighbor was quick to respond.

"Well, it just seems like at some point or another, all of us 'round here done had some hand in helping Daniel come up. Family is family, and I understand that. But if Daniel was living alone, if he needed help, why not reach out to somebody and let them know? Why not ask us for help?"

"Our business ain't everybody's business," Aunt Josie snapped again.

"It's okay, Auntie," I said, softly. Everybody got quiet.

"I moved out into my own place a while ago—almost a year. When I moved out, we were able to put Daniel into an assisted living community across town. It seemed like a pretty nice place. He liked the nurses there. Everybody was feeling a little weighed down with responsibility, but also like we couldn't devote the attention to Daniel that he needed. So we decided it was the best option for his care and safety, as well as for us to be able to make some of the life improvements we were looking to make."

"So, you just left him there."

"We didn't leave him anywhere. He lived there," I said.

"And now he's not living at all. Do you still feel like that was a good decision?"

"You are OUT of line!" Aunt Nell yelled.

"I've got it, Auntie," I said.

"Listen, Daniel lived with me longer than anybody. I was the closest person to him. You think I don't feel this? Feel regret? Like I don't think about every single thing that could have been done differently so that this didn't happen? I missed him when he moved, but I thought I was doing the right thing. I never claimed to know everything.

"The doctors said he died of natural causes. At nineteen? I don't believe it. Can't believe it, but what can we do? He didn't have health issues; there were never any signs of complications. You're asking me if I feel like moving him was a good decision. You're really maybe asking me if I feel like Daniel died from a broken heart. From loneliness. Maybe it's true. But my brother had a hard life. Even though he smiled all the way through it, his life was *so hard*.

"And I'm happy that he doesn't have to deal with this anymore. This drama. The trifles. The pain of only being able to see so far but knowing there's more over the horizon. I don't have to care what you think about my family.

"But right here, right now, don't disrespect my brother's memory by accusing the people that loved him the most, and who *he* loved the most, of negligence. We may be a lot of things. But we've never been that. We've never been that."

Everyone was quiet. Our neighbors kept their eyes on their plates, some of them dragging their fork's teeth across the surface. Aunt Josie and Aunt Nell were red with embarrassment and crying, their husbands at their sides, consoling them.

It was silent for a couple more moments. I'm not

quite sure why, but I just started talking after a while. I hardly knew what I was saying.

"Aside from the last year, I had been with my brother his whole life … my whole life. The parts that mattered, anyway.

"You know how most kids are scared of the dark? Daniel never was. It always confused me, because there he was, just as simple as can be—you think he'd be scared at everything unexplainable, acts of God … but no. He'd sit in the dark, with thunder and lightning outside, clapping and grinning, having the best time in the world. When I asked him if he was scared, he'd shake his head and smile."

"Daniel didn't see darkness as we have grown to know darkness. He didn't see goblins or monsters … fear … the unknown. He didn't see loneliness in the dark. Sometimes I think he was better off than all of us in that respect.

"That's how my brother lived. You might call it ignorant or oblivious, but I say that what we took for a disability in Daniel actually turned out to be one of his greatest abilities. He focused on what really mattered. That's something I learned from him and try to practice. I think … I think we should all practice it now. I know we all want to remember Daniel in a positive way. All of you had a hand in raising him. So do that. Remember him by what matters. That's what I'm going to do.

"I'm gonna remember the secrets we used to share under our covers on those rainy nights … walking to school together, explaining why Marco couldn't walk with him anymore. I'll remember picking up dandelions in Ms. Pryor's backyard and blowing the seeds all around. I'll remember dressing him up for junior prom and standing in the back of the party embarrassed because he wanted to dance in the middle of the floor in the spotlight." A chuckle tumbled out of me. "What a night.

"I'll remember taking care of my brother when he got the flu at sixteen, and it seemed like the end of the world. He couldn't understand why he couldn't breathe and his head hurt so bad.

"I'll remember living with him up until his first day at the home. I walked out of that room toward the door, and right before I got outside good I turned around, and he stood there just smiling. Smiling, you know, like … like he knew I was worried, scared to death. Like he knew I thought I was making the wrong decision, but smiling like he was telling me everything would be all right.

"It lifted a burden off me," I barely coughed out. I was crying uncontrollably at this point.

"I didn't know what was going to happen. If keeping him with me would have kept him living, I would have kept him with me forever. I swear, I would have. But when I saw that smile … I felt like I knew something I had worried about knowing before. I knew my brother had had a life. He lived. He had time ... all the time he needed, even though that time ain't but a fraction of what people like us hope to have.

"Daniel wasn't people like us, though. He was our people, but he wasn't people like us. The only thing that hurts now is that I told him I'd never leave him ... that I'd be there for him forever. But you know what? Me and Daniel, we had our forever. We had our little forever."

I figure I was talking too much or crying too much, or maybe both, because Quila came up and hugged my neck tight then said a few words to the guests to make them get up and start leaving. We left soon after that, and I hopped back in Quila's car even though our family wanted me to ride in the limousine with them. It was just me and Quila, and the air in the car was thick. My stomach turned somersaults, and my head was heavy and hollow. Quila rolled down the window.

"You know ... that was really beautiful ... that stuff you said about Daniel back there," she said.

"I was just talking."

"Yeah? Yeah ... well, I hope they were listening ... I really hope they were listening."

Quila and I swerved around the back of Aunt

Josie's house and parked in the grass next to the patio. I don't know if she saw my hands trembling, but I wasn't ready to go in. Quila took her phone and plugged it into the radio and started playing old songs. Songs like Mama used to play on Sundays when we would clean the house.

I never did clean much on account of I wasn't very good at it, and Mama didn't want me messing anything up. But hearing that music and Mama singing along while everybody was cleaning their part used to make me feel good inside. Made me feel calm, like nothing could go wrong. I was thankful that Quila knew that, and even more thankful for her remembering in that moment.

Ferguson

The last time I had seen Quila before Daniel's funeral was in Ferguson, Missouri, a little while after the police murdered Mike Brown, sometime after Attorney General Holder announced the Civil Rights investigation.

Everybody thinks if you're my kind of *special* that you don't have feelings. Can't comprehend emotions, empathize with others—stuff like that. I may not be the most aware, but I always had feelings. And I had them hurt so many ways growing up that I could always recognize pain. I'd feel downright sorry too, knowing what it's like and all. Ferguson pulled me in that way.

I should have expected that Quila would be there. We got so used to Quila being in another world that sometimes, I forgot I knew her. I never forgot I knew her *really*, but I didn't concern myself with all the details of her life. I didn't understand half of them. I don't know. We knew Quila was gone, and she was happy. That was normally enough.

It also could be that I didn't fully understand what her job was about at that point. Either way, she was down there in a group that was trying to help the black businessfolk in Ferguson maintain their businesses through the crisis, send out the right messages to the public, and not get in trouble with the law.

I saw Quila's name and contact information on a resource flyer people in the community were passing out. My first instinct was to tag along with her, but I knew I would be too shy to talk to all those smart people she was with. I didn't want to embarrass her. I went to the marches and listened to the speeches by church deacons, students, and activists. It felt good to be a part of something, even if nobody particularly knew I was there.

During one of the rallies, I was standing between a little girl and an old man. The little girl to my left had on pink shoes with a Velcro strap. She couldn't have been more than six or seven years old. She had on a pink bubble coat; it was the time of year where the nights had begun to get chilly in the Midwest. She stomped her feet hard into the pavement as she marched and kept up with the chants of the crowd.

She held the hands of her freedom fighter parents, emulating their every gesture. Her demeanor, her motions—genetic in their congruence.

I watched her intently, a little liberator-in-training, already more advanced than so many people who wander through this life, unaware of the devices set in place to control us, stifle us, keep us underfoot. As I watched her, I wondered what my life would be like if I had those type of genetics. If Mama was anybody other than who she was, who would I be? Could I ever have been a freedom fighter, the fervent passion and righteousness sewed into my DNA at conception? Or was I always destined to be me? To be this? Across all times and spaces, under a glass bell, looking out into a distorted world, with a distorted face to boot.

The air was thick. Heavier than your everyday humidity. Thick with tension and fear. Rage and anxiety. We were all waiting for something to happen, but none of us were quite sure what it would be.

Each step felt like what should have been a milestone. You held your breath as you put each foot down, only to realize that you would have to take another step to achieve anything.

Stomp. Wait. Breathe, barely. The old man beside me tried to strike up a conversation through the call of the crowd.

"You're here alone," he said.

"What?" I cupped my hand to my ear.

"I said, you're here alone. I am too."

"Oh. Yes."

"Are you a lawyer?" he asked me.

"Me? No. I'm just … I'm just a guy."

He chuckled. "Me too, fella. Me too. Just us guys out here today, then."

I smiled awkwardly and faced forward again.

"My wife used to come with me," he said.

"What?"

"I said, my *wife*. Bless her heart and rest her soul, she used to come with me. You know, to the marches."

"Is she dead?" I asked.

"She is."

"I'm sorry."

"Well, we can't live forever. She would be happy, though. Here, now. Seeing all these young people. It's really a shame what has happened. But she'd be proud that we're not being quiet."

"Yeah? Yeah … well, quiet doesn't solve problems."

"Loud hasn't either, historically," he quipped.

I got confused. I didn't know if he wanted me to agree with him or to debate him. I felt like maybe the answer was somewhere in the middle. Or maybe he didn't want anything at all. I didn't like being confused, so I decided to be quiet.

"Do you think it will ever end?" he asked.

"Will what end?"

"The killing. The racism. They stamp us out like roaches, man."

"I, um … I'm not sure. I never thought about it before."

"It's important to think about. Would you be here if you believed it would never end?"

"What?"

"I said, would you be here—here, in Missouri. Marching. If you believed—"

"What?"

I motioned that I couldn't hear him over the chant of the crowd. I could hear him fine, but he was making me uncomfortable. I didn't want to answer questions. I didn't want to march anymore. My head was pounding, and I was getting short of breath. There were people surrounding me on every side, and as I slid further and further into the crowd away from the old man, my breathing grew more and more shallow.

I could feel my legs getting wobbly and my palms sweating. My heart sprinted. I searched for a way out of the crowd, but I couldn't find one. I wanted to kneel down and let everybody pass me, but I knew I would get trampled.

I put my hands over my ears to drown out the noise. Someone tugged on my shirt from the back. I twisted side to side, trying to yank myself out of their tight grip. I twisted and shook harder and harder but couldn't get loose. They pulled me around, and I turned to face them, nearly colliding.

Quila.

"Hey! Are you okay?" she called.

There were tears in my eyes as I shook my head.

"Come on. Let's go this way."

Quila led me through the crowd to the sidewalk, out of the way of the protesters. We sat down outside a restaurant that was closed, on the benches that were used for parties who wait for tables. I wiped the tears from my eyes with my right sleeve while Quila rubbed my left hand.

"This a li'l better?"

"Yeah," I said. "Thank you … I just got, uh … I got overwhelmed back there."

"It's overwhelming. All of this is. Collective emotion is so powerful. It's volatile, too, though."

"Yeah, I can see what you mean."

We sat in silence for a while, watching the crowd march by. The auburn sun slid behind the horizon. It looked like it was a thousand miles away from us, but its warmth was much closer. I sat with my hands resting on my thighs, and Quila rubbed my hand until it melted into my leg. I closed my eyes. Protesters chanted in the distance, the birds chattered even farther away, and indistinguishable sounds murmured beyond.

The birds sounded like the ones back home.

I thought about home as a place, a concept. Ferguson was home to many people. And on their streets, in their neighborhood, there was fire and glass. Outside of houses, as children slept, there was unrest. In a quiet, country town, not quite unlike my own, a boy was murdered.

"Come on," Quila said.

I slept on the couch in her hotel room that night, even though I had my own room.

I dreamed that I was marching. Marching for a

long time. There wasn't a huge crowd though, just me and a few other people.

We were all spread out, and I couldn't see them, but I knew they were there. Our footsteps hit the ground at all different times, so instead of an army marching, we sounded like a stampede. Beads of sweat formed on my neck. My heart beat quickly. I wanted to run, but I couldn't see ahead of me. The road was shrouded in a heavy, foggy mist. I kept my same pace, not knowing what else to do.

That was the whole dream. I marched and marched. Maybe for days, maybe years. I never stopped or turned or ran into anybody else. I just kept going. And when I woke up, I wasn't sure why. I'm still not sure.

The next day was community service. It was something Quila's company had organized for the kids in the city, some sort of back-to-school festival for supplies and book bags. Things that stress parents out and make them thankful somebody else offers to take care of them.

I was organizing bags and supplies most of the morning. It was soothing to turn my brain off and do a menial, repetitive task. I knew that kids and adults would rush in, trying by any means to get the best supplies first. I would need to find a quiet corner to protect my peace.

The rush came, but it wasn't how I thought it

would be. The mood was somber, even among the little ones. People filed in with solemn smiles and soft steps. They took backpacks and notebooks, thanked the organizers, and didn't mill around for too long.

A couple of mothers shared their worries about the beginning of school. Kids of all ages would be walking, alone. To school, to the bus stops, to afterschool activities. Who would be next? Who would be the next Mike Brown? The entire city was quiet, on the heels of one tragedy, bracing for the next. The collective emotion was as fluid as a wave that swept across Ferguson with each new piece of information. Rage. Exasperation. Primal fear. You never really knew what sort of day it was going to be. And that was the scariest thing of all.

I didn't see Quila again for a while after that. One of her assistants took me to the airport that evening so that I could catch my flight. I came back to my small job in my small town with a different sort of collective consciousness.

Beyond the city limits of my hometown, nothing was real. Shops would open in the morning and close at night. Mr. Parker would play his guitar down at the BBQ restaurant Thursday evenings for tips. Far away, there was a dead boy, a city on fire, and a world crashing down around people just like us. But they weren't like us. Because they weren't real. They were just stories. Stories from far, far away.

half-moons

I did my deep thinking late at night, in bed. My mind rewound through the day: Daniel's funeral, the meal, the family. Then everything. Everything flooded in. Different pains from different times. I began to get angry, on the verge of tears, thinking why? *Why did nobody ever tell me?* There had to be someone who knew about me. You know, who really knew.

There had to be someone who could explain to a child that his brain isn't made like everybody else's and he's not as good as them because of it. He's not special. He's not different. He's not unique. He's broken. And his life is going to be hard and painful because nobody wants to hold broken pieces of glass. They either put them down or throw them out. The holding isn't worth the risk of getting cut. Somebody had to be able to explain that to a young boy. But, then again, maybe they didn't want to. Maybe they couldn't bring themselves to do it. Maybe they were cowards. Cowards that thought it might be better for this boy to grow up not knowing what to call all these problems.

Maybe they thought if it didn't have a name, it wouldn't seem real. I wish I could tell them, all of them, all of the people that *must* have known and refused to say anything. I wish I could tell them how hard it was. How hard it still is. I wish I could tell them that just because a person doesn't understand what it means to be broken doesn't mean they can't tell they aren't whole.

I got angry and cried and cursed the world and then cried some more and felt sorry for myself. I cried until I didn't know what to do anymore, and then I finally put on my pajamas and laid back down to sleep, because tomorrow would be a new day, and what else could I do but get ready?

As I lay in bed, I couldn't shake the thoughts from before. There are always secrets. We reckon they will protect the ones we love, but I can't be so sure anymore. It feels like we're all setting each other up for failure. Trapping ourselves inside a taboo that doesn't exist.

I used to believe Mama guided me, simple me, through the dark while I was blindfolded, holding my hand and calling out to me. My only stumbles came from my uneasy feet. But one day, Mama was gone. No more hands, no more voice. I took my blindfold off, but my eyes ain't adjusting. They just ain't adjusting.

I wonder how the world would be different if we weren't so scared to talk about the things that make us fearful. The things we don't understand. The whole world, everybody but me, knew I had these problems and nobody ever sat me down and taught me how to live. Nobody ever tried. I'm stuck now. I never know if I'm right or wrong. My heart and my brain are archenemies, and sometimes I don't know if it's me making decisions. But what can I do? Who can I trust? Who in the world knows me better than I know me?

In the morning, there would be Sunday service and breakfast after, and then some family time before people went their separate ways. It was the same after every funeral. I longed for the whole ordeal to be over, but I knew I would be sad when Quila left.

***

The aroma of sausage and eggs woke me. My head was pounding and I felt dizzy. I lay in bed for a while, trying to squint the pain out through my ears. I grabbed the bottle of water from my nightstand and took a few large gulps. Why had I been so upset the night before? The mood still pulled me down in certain places, like Christmas tree ornaments hanging on the branches. My shoulders felt heavy; my eyes, tired. My hands trembled as I grabbed my robe and headed to the bathroom.

I had been nauseated all weekend and even the week leading up to the funeral, but who wouldn't be? Even though the services were over, something felt unfinished. I couldn't quite place the feeling. Maybe anxiety. Would more conversations happen about Daniel? I was on edge, waiting for something to happen. *Wanting* something to happen so the stress of anticipation would dissolve. But what? I had no idea.

I don't know what I wanted people to do now that my brother was dead, but we all knew things weren't the same, so why should they feel the same? People know how to act like nothing has changed, even if it has. It's cold. Everything would continue on as it had. Maybe that's necessary, but it just didn't feel right.

Black people have been put through so much. We have become so accepting of tragedy. I used to think about how bad we struggled. Seemed like it could never end. And I would wonder, if we ever found peace, how black could we really be? I'm not sure what else is behind the skin, but struggle. No matter what kind of black you are or where you're from, we all share that. We was taught to be proud of that, but I'm not sure it's enough anymore. It made me sad because I figured even if we wanted better in our hearts, our legs would keep walking us around in circles.

I had never thought too hard about somebody leaving the town, in a car or in a casket, but now it pained me. And I felt that pain not only for Daniel but for all the other families who lost someone while the rest of us just kept right on living. The more I thought, the sicker I felt. I didn't want to talk to anybody. There were guests and a few distant relatives still in the house—I could hear them outside the bathroom chatting and chuckling. I had to get away.

After I cleaned myself up, I snuck out the side door and ambled down the winding path that connected to the main road. The pine trees stood strong up against the wind, but the leaves and pebbles littering the main road got thrown all about. I didn't too much know where I was going, just that I needed a little fresh air before sitting down with everybody at breakfast.

As I walked, I thought about Daniel. Quila. Our neighbors. I passed the houses that used to be filled with folks I knew. Folks who either done gone on to something bigger and better or fell down into something much worse. Either way, when they were out of this place, mentally or physically, they were gone. Out of sight, out of mind. It's the only way the town could absolve itself of guilt or responsibility to improve. Because we never fully acknowledge when people leave, for better or worse, our world stays small; the community continues sustaining itself off tradition. Nothing more is needed than all the things we already have.

That's what we liked to tell ourselves, anyway.

I was almost past the pale blue house with the

cracking foundation and off-white stone columns before Mr. Len called out to me. He had known my siblings and me since we were babies. The quiet old man pretty much kept to himself other than the necessary grocery shopping trips he had to make (which he sometimes outsourced to neighborhood kids for a couple of bucks). The only way anyone ever really saw him was as he was right now, sitting on the porch in a rocking chair nearly as old as him.

"Alright, now." He nodded.

I nodded back and kept meandering.

He rocked and sipped from his glass of sweet tea. Sometimes he'd trade his sweet tea in for a glass of lemonade, but never too many days in a row. We were always taught old folks are supposed to be wise, but a lot of people in town figured Mr. Len was crazy on account of some of the comments he would make.

One day, Mr. Len stopped me and Mama on our way to the river and told Mama that I was a smart boy. She twisted her mouth up in confusion and tried not to be rude. But the more he insisted, the more offended she got.

When we got home later that night, Mama kept fussing about how Mr. Len "took her for a fool," and "thought he was funny." I knew why he had said I was smart, but I had never told Mama. She stayed mad at Mr. Len for some months before she started returning his quiet nods on her way walking to the river.

Mr. Len started reckoning I was smart from one day when I was little. I was playing by the river past his house. It was one of those summer evenings that took its good time crawling into twilight. The days never ended then. I was trying to skip stones and catch salamanders. Mama had told me not to go alone, but Marco didn't feel like coming with me, so I snuck away.

I splashed around for a long time. By the time I realized how long I had been gone, I could barely see the black side of my hands by the light of the moon. I rushed up out of the riverbed and bolted down the street, back toward home. Mr. Len was outside rocking, as usual.

"You alright there, now?" he asked.

I slowed down and peered through the dark.

"Uh, yessir. I just got to get home. I ain't know it was so late."

"Mmph. I reckon it done got mighty dark."

"Yessir."

"Come on up here. I'll call your mama and let her know you're on your way so she can save what

85

little worry she might have left."

I walked up the steps and into the house. I stood in the middle of a living room, and Mr. Len walked through the kitchen and into the dining room to search through stacks and stacks of loose papers and magazines and books. After a few minutes, he held up a slip of paper that had several phone numbers on it.

"Which one of these is your mama's number?"

I pointed to the correct one, and he started to dial.

The house was littered with all types of knickknacks, almost like Mr. Len was packing to move or searching for something he couldn't find. They weren't regular knickknacks though.

He had some strange, tribal-looking masks, longs scrolls of paper with different languages written on them, small figurines in the shape of men, women, and animals that I had never seen before. A few notebooks were stacked up on the kitchen table. I opened one up as Mr. Len walked back through the kitchen into the living room.

"What you rummaging through over here?" he inquired.

I closed the book quickly and put my hands behind my back. "Nothing."

He grinned. "You know what's in there?" I shook my head.

"Stories. All kinds of 'em. You like stories?"

I shrugged and twisted side to side while looking down at the floor.

"Where did all these little statues come from?" I asked.

"All around the world," he answered. "Come on. I will walk you to the fork in the road where we can see your street. Your mama was worried sick about you. You got it in for yourself when you get home."

We walked most of the way in silence. It was a calm night. Calm and cloudy, and we couldn't see too many stars.

"You know what that is up there?" Mr. Len pointed up to the sky.

I looked straight up at the moon. It was a half moon, the dark clouds circling around it like a ceremonial dance. It was glowing bright as I had ever seen.

"That's the moon."

"Yessir, it is. Beautiful, ain't it?" We kept walking without talking for some time longer.

"Month almost over. You know, they say when the moon is cut in half like that at the end of the month, it's a time for release and forgiveness. Maybe your mama won't be so mad. What you think?"

I wrinkled my brow and I looked up in the sky again.

"Say there, what's the matter?"

I had something I wanted to say, but I had gotten used to keeping quiet on account of trying not to embarrass Mama.

"Say there, little fella."

"Well, that ain't half a moon."

"What you mean, boy? It's just as plain as the nose on your face up there."

"I don't know, Mr. Len."

"What don't you know? You can only see half of it, right?"

"Well, yeah. But that *is* what I mean. We can only *see* half, but the other half still there. The moon ain't half or cut in half. That moon ain't no half. One side just dark."

Mr. Len rubbed his chin and pondered my words for a moment before letting out a *hmm*.

"So, I don't know how much forgiving Mama gonna do. Long as that whole moon up there in the sky, she gonna be my whole Mama."

Mr. Len let out a muffled chuckle and patted me on the back. We made it to the fork in the road, my street about thirty yards away. As soon as I turned on it, my house would be three down on the left.

"Well, thanks, Mr. Len. I'm sure Mama awful thankful."

"Mmph."

I started down the street, but I didn't make it too far before Mr. Len called after me.

"It's hard to see things for what they are, sometimes," he shouted through the dark. He glowed in the moonlight. The air on that street was quiet, our voices the only sounds. "The *all* of what they are. Most people can't do it. But you're special. You got a special kind of sight. Use it."

"Yessir," I said, and kept on toward my house. I had no idea what he was talking about.

***

I missed breakfast.

I came back inside to a quiet house, with different

family members scattered around, throwing clothes into bags or saying their goodbyes before they hit the road. There was some doctor on the television in the main den, talking at Aunt Josie while she hummed and knitted what looked like it was headed toward a scarf.

I wondered if anything the doctor was saying made it through Aunt Josie's ears to her brain.

> *Our community, and lack thereof, doesn't understand the depth or complexity of grief, guilt, abandonment, depression, lack of self-worth, etc. They just don't get it. We, as a whole, are so damaged that our pain has blinded us from the pain of others. We're not able to extend empathy or true understanding and acceptance to others ... we dismiss everything with veiled eyes and deaf ears ... we've lost our humanity ...*

"Auntie," I said.

Aunt Josie jerked around to face me.

"Boy! I didn't even hear you in here. Where you been? You missed breakfast."

"I know. I took a walk."

"Mmm. Well, half the family done gone. Few still millin' around here. Wasn't nothin' but useless chatter over breakfast anyhow. I probably should have taken a walk myself."

I nodded. "What you doin' knittin' that scarf with it so hot out?"

"By the time it's cold enough for it, I'll wish I'd have knitted it, now don't ya think?"

She had a point. I walked out of the den and into the kitchen to find Quila sitting at the table, poring over some documents. She had music playing from her phone as she thumbed through the paperwork.

"Hey, Qu—" I started.

She held her palm up and closed her eyes. When the baseline dropped on the jazz song she was listening to, she snapped and moved her shoulders and swayed to the rhythm of the music. I half-smiled. Quila had always loved jazz. And dancing too. When Quila grooved, nobody around wanted to do much of anything except watch her. She was just so smooth. You'd get more enjoyment watching her move than you could ever get dancing on your own. Quila was a diamond in the dark.

"A Love Supreme," she said.

"We used to listen to this on the way to your games."

"We sure did." She smiled.

"How was this morning?"

"A lot of words. A lot of talking. Very little communicating, for the most part."

"What about?"

Quila raised her right hand slightly, with her palm facing the ceiling, and rotated her wrist a couple of times. A Quila way of saying *nothing worth saying*.

"Got it."

"Where were you?"

"Walkin'. Lost track of time. I saw Mr. Len."

"*Really?!* Gosh, I haven't seen him in ages. Is he doing well? Still drinking tea? Oh, gosh. Do you remember Ujima?"

"Ha ha. Yeah, he's doing alright. Same old Mr. Len ... Say, Quila?"

"Say."

"I know I'm just now gettin' out on my own and all. But uh, I guess I was walkin' around today just thinkin' ... I was thinkin' about leavin'...you know? Really leavin'."

Quila smiled at me with her eyes. "Honey, you been gone a long time."

Ujima

The first time I ever remember it being cold in our town was around the same time Mr. Len called Mama to ask if Quila and I could run to the store for him. Mama tried to send us directly from the house, but Mr. Len insisted we stop by his place first. He said he didn't have his list handy and would need time to find it. Besides, he wanted to give us the money ahead of time.

When we got there, Mr. Len let us inside. A strong aroma of apples and cinnamon wafted from his usual tea mug. He offered us glasses, and we sat down to sip while he walked into the kitchen to shuffle around in the drawers. The cider was warm inside my chest; I dug a cozy spot for myself into the couch and breathed deeply.

As we sipped, Quila and I giggled about the figurines and fancy blankets all around. I had told her all about the last time I was in Mr. Len's house. She said that some of the stuff in Mr. Len's house looked like it came from places she had read about in school, but she doubted that he had ever truly been that far away from our town.

Nobody from our town ever went that far. At least nobody who ever came back to tell about it.

Mr. Len was taking a long time shuffling through those drawers. We turned and noticed that he had left the kitchen. It sounded like he was moving around in one of the back rooms. Quila had finished her cider and headed into the kitchen to return her mug. After putting it in the sink, she opened up the refrigerator.

"Mr. Len, do you have anything to snack on while we wait—"

Mr. Len appeared in the doorway, holding a large book covered in black cloth. As he unwrapped the cloth, red and green fabric appeared underneath.

"Mr. Len, you sure do have a good many groceries already."

Mr. Len eyed the open refrigerator and grunted.

"I reckon so. Come sit down and take a look at this."

Quila and Mr. Len came back over to the couch where I was. He sat between us and opened up the book. Inside were strange symbols and more words in a language I didn't understand.

The colors were brilliant, and each page of the big book was filled top to bottom with pictures and illustrations. I had never seen a book with only black people in it. Mr. Len scrolled past the first several pages of the book and landed on the one he had been looking for.

"This is the third day of Kwanzaa."

"That African holiday?" Quila asked.

"It's not African; it's for black people. Black people like us."

"But the words are in Swahili, right?"

"Mmm hmm. But it's not *just* for African people to celebrate. They use these African principles to help black people around the world celebrate."

"What are we celebratin'?" I blurted out.

Quila was unconvinced. "That's not what they told us in school."

"Oh, yeah? Well, I reckon when you graduate and go on, you'll learn a lot of things they didn't tell you in school." Mr. Len smiled slyly. "We are celebrating ourselves, my boy. All that we have done and all that we are capable of doing."

I saw Quila's mouth turn up and her eyes squint after Mr. Len's comment, a face that meant she was offended but would hold her tongue out of respect.

"Y'all missed the first two days."

"We don't celebrate this," I said.

"That's why y'all missed the first two days," he fired back. Mr. Len had a mouth slick like Quila's.

"The first day is about unity and the second day is about self-determination—living as your true self, basically. I been debating calling your mama to get her to let y'all come over here and learn something for the last two days, but today ... today, you couldn't afford to miss. Ujima."

"What's Ah-gee-mah?" I asked.

Quila leaned over a little to look at the picture in the book. It was like a mural, spanning the entire foldout of the two pages it covered. Black people were everywhere, doing everything.

Some were working, some playing. Some were talking, others listening. Teaching, building, consoling, crying, eating, praying. The setting looked like an African town, but some people were dressed up in suits or fancy robes with colors. I had never seen anything about Africa that looked nice before. Always poor and beat down; struggling. Quila and I got lost in the details of the mural. Lost in sonder. Each of the little women and men had a story, a purpose. Children, parents, a job, goals, dreams. I could feel it all through the mural. And I wanted to know every detail.

"Collective work and responsibility—that's what

Ujima means—to build and maintain our community *together*. And make our brothers' and sisters' problems our problems, and to solve them *together*."

"I can't solve Quila's problems; they're too hard," I complained. Quila laughed.

"Child, who are you tellin'?"

"You'd be surprised at what you could do," said Mr. Len. "But we're not necessarily talkin' about school problems. It could be anything that comes up in your life. And it doesn't just have to be your brothers and sisters at home. All black people should treat each other like brothers and sisters."

I was confused, but Mama would tell me not to say something stupid if I wasn't sure if it was smart, so I was quiet and sipped on my starting-to-get-cold cider.

"Mr. Len, I never heard these words pronounced," said Quila.

"Probably ain't too many people around these parts speak Swahili. I know I don't. But black people all over the world use these principles to guide their lives. Kwanzaa is only once a year, so there ain't too much other time or reason for folks to be pronouncing these words, I figure."

I could see Quila thinking hard about what Mr.

Len was telling us.

"It's kinda like working, together, huh?" she asked.

"That's exactly what it's like. But not just on a school project or at your job. Black people got dealt a bad hand over here in America. There's *always* some way that somebody needs help. And on the other side, always somebody that has a way to help. That's what this is about."

"Why doesn't everybody feel this way?" she asked.

Mr. Len chuckled. "I have asked myself the same thing many, many times, young lady. I figure some folks don't see it. And some folks just don't care to see it. But we can only do what we can do."

"Seems like if all the black people in the world could live like this, we would be better off, huh?"

"Sure does seem like it, doesn't it?"

Quila nodded and leaned over Mr. Len to read more in the book. A lump formed in my throat, and I started to tap my foot as Quila giggled and chatted with Mr. Len about the pictures.

"Quila, it's getting late."

Mr. Len responded before she could. "I reckon you're right."

"Do you still need us to go to the store for you?" Quila asked.

"I think I got all I need," said Mr. Len. "But take this book. Don't tell your mama you got it from me. Keep reading on it. I think you'll like it."

We got up and headed toward the door. Right before we crossed the threshold, Quila turned around to thank Mr. Len for the book.

"How'd you learn about all this stuff anyway?" she asked.

Mr. Len turned around and looked at all the foreign artifacts in his den. He forced a smile.

"A long time ago, I traveled the world. Country to country, fighting for the flag. I learned a lot from that. One of them travels, I met a woman, … reckon I fell in love. I learned a lot from her, too. We traveled on and on after that, together. I brought all the little pieces from everywhere right back here."

"Well … why they never taught us nothing like this in school?"

"Lotta people don't know their own history. Sad enough, sometimes the people that *do* know don't want you to know."

Quila looked Mr. Len directly in the eyes. I shifted my weight, considering what he had said. I didn't fully understand what he was referencing. Fighting, flags, traveling. I moved to ask a question, but Quila touched my arm lightly with her index and middle finger. A Quila way of saying *not right now*.

"Thanks, Mr. Len. I like this stuff. We appreciate the cider. We're gonna get going now."

Mr. Len gave each of us two dollars to present to Mama as "change" for the groceries that we didn't buy. Quila was intent on keeping Mr. Len's secret, but I wanted to tell. I didn't get a book, and I didn't have fun either. It seemed like he was trying to call us over there just to do something he knew Mama wouldn't like. Quila sensed my frustration. She knew everything about me then, even more than I knew. And she knew just how to get me.

"I'll give you my two bucks if you don't tell Mama."

It seemed fair enough.

saying goodbye

Quila lay with the back of her head on my chest, looking up at the ceiling. She had done this ever since I was a little kid, whenever we were close to parting ways. We didn't have to talk or anything. Sometimes all the unspoken feelings from the day could get processed right there in silence as we lay.

It made me feel like I was the big brother, to have her lay on me. It gave me a sense of power, like I could protect her, though I never knew from what. And even if I did, I'm sure Quila could handle most anything alone before ever needing *my* help. Even still, it was nice to have her lay on me. It felt like old times.

"Everybody's heart sounds different," she said. "It's like your own little song."

She was her very own shade of perfect.

"When are you coming back?" I asked her.

"Not really sure."

"Not much reason," I added.

Quila shrugged and kept looking at the ceiling.

She used to imagine that all the indentations in the sheetrock were stars in the galaxy. She'd count them until she fell asleep.

"But you. Leaving, huh?" she asked. "I mean, I'm happy to hear it, but whe—"

"I ain't thought about it too much. You know I'm just now getting out of this house, let alone the town. But I don't know … this weekend … I just feel like it's time."

"Past time," Quila added. "What about your doctor? You going to be able to find a new one you like?"

"They had me taking something for a little while, but I didn't feel too good on it. I just take melatonin to sleep now. I have high days and low days, but at least I'm in control. I'll probably be able to manage okay until I can find somebody else."

"Oh, God. Control." Quila laughed. "As if any of us are ever. I'm proud of you, babe. You have to do what's right for you. And Daniel, bless his heart. But you can truly focus on yourself now."

I got up and started pacing.

"What if I don't know what's best for me, Quila?"

"Hmm. I don't think anybody ever truly does until

they figure out what's *not* best for them first. You done already did the hard part, baby."

"Yeah, but what's out there for me? The world ain't built for ..."

"Ain't built for who? Who say so?"

Quila was starting to get defensive. My ears were getting hot. I looked at the ground and felt my palms well up with moisture.

"Never mind," I muttered.

"Oh, no. Imma mind!" Quila said aggressively. She was standing up now. I watched her finger push into my chest as she scolded me. "You can do *anything* these other people can do. You done let them talk you into sitting around here like you can't be anything, got you down on yourself, and I'm sick of it. You deserve so much better! And you act like nobody knows any better than you as soon as they try to tell—"

"Tell me WHAT, Quila?! Not the truth. It ain't the truth! It ain't never been. Everybody pities me. Feels sorry. They called me special my whole life. Nothing they say now can change that. Nothing can change the fact that I've never been right."

Quila tilted my chin up with her hand and looked into my eyes. Hers were small. Beady and brown.

They saw through me, to the core. They saw everything within me. Quila hugged herself to my chest, cheek pressed against my sternum.

"All you know … all you are … everything that you have ever been … is *so* much more than they knew or could articulate. Than I could, or Mama could, or even you could. You have always been undeniably more. *That* is what's special. And that is the truest truth I know."

I kept hugging Quila, and she kept hugging me. I cried, but not too hard like I did when I was alone. Quila used her sleeves to wipe her face as she was hugging me, so I believe she was crying too. I had never had to think about what was next; I was always told to be happy—I figured I was lucky— with what I had been given. But everything was different now.

The unknown is a terrifying magnet. My stomach flipped and twirled at the inexactness of it all. But I knew it was right. After spending so long not knowing the difference between what should happen and what just so happens to happen, I knew what was right. And all the proof I needed was in Quila's words and embrace.

***

Nobody had ever talked to me about comorbidities. Latency. Personality or mood disorders. Mental illness. Disability. You were either right or you weren't. You were off. Touched. Special. Did my family and neighbors even know what those words really meant?

I sit and wonder how different things would have been if somebody could have told me who I was; what was wrong with me. Then I think ... would anything have been different at all? You don't get to choose your book, but you *can* choose how you tell your story.

Times like these, I remember my guidance counselor from school and the man-counselor who came to visit. They had an idea. Maybe the right idea. It's funny, but it's also sad, how you can be so close to the truth, to your salvation, and never know it. I wish I could have known what they meant all those years ago.

I see now that they were trying to be helpful. But there's only so much you can affect in your little corner of the world, especially when the people that need your help can't or won't meet you halfway. I wish we had known good enough to meet them halfway. I wonder how many other little black boys and girls they tried to save. I wonder if they did save any of them. I sure hope so.

***

I once dreamed I was running through a field filled with butterflies. Orange butterflies. They scattered as I passed through the field with my arms outstretched. But they all came back down and landed after I had passed. The butterflies covered me, and I saw everything. I knew everything. I was everything. And it was all true.

Tree

I wasn't born with tough skin; I was made like this. You try being anything different for long enough and you'll realize people just don't get it sometimes. Most of the time. I read people like books, but not everybody is like that. I try not to be mad at them for what they don't know or can't understand. There's plenty I don't know and never been able to understand, no matter how much I tried.

My name is Kamani. It means tree. I was named by my sister, Aquila. Sometimes I feel like I failed her. She thought our neighborhood needed trees. Tall, strong forces of nature, providing shade for the weary and fruit for the hungry, air for the ones choking on the smoggy culture of the town. It was very poetic of her. My sister wanted a Great Oak in this neighborhood. But instead she got me.

When a tree is growing and it encounters something that gets in the way of its growth, it has three options: it can stop growing, grow away from the object, or grow around it. Everything that has happened in my life—most times I wish I would have stopped growing.

Wish I was laying somewhere quiet, peaceful, like Marco. Like Daniel. But I grew around everything.

I didn't try; I just did. You ever see them trees grow around something? It'll be small, like a street sign or an old stake in the ground. Me and Derrick found a tree that had grown around an old abandoned bike when we was little. Roots deep, crawling straight up through the tire spokes to the trunk—bent them spokes and everything. But that's how a lot of trees grow.

That's how I grew. Through the crazy, the trauma, the depression. You look at me and you might not know right off. But you take another look and you can see my roots shooting up through the spokes. You can tell I ain't quite right.

I guess that's one thing Quila ain't figure before she named me; the torment trees have to grow through. The rain and the ice, the heat and the cold … they die and come back again. Get chopped down, spring new life from odd angles.

All manner of creatures make a home out of a tree. Eat off it, sleep in it. And the tree just keeps growing, almost like it don't know no better. Almost like it can't help it. Just keep reaching up higher and higher toward the sky. Tryin' to grab one of them clouds it can't never hold.

And even if it could, then what? The endurance is

a curse. The strength is a curse. The unwavering, subconscious instinct to survive is a curse if you gotta grow how I grew. But it ain't nothing we can do about it. We get what names we get, and for whatever reason. Sometimes I wonder if Quila realizes that she was the Great Oak.

Times like these I'll stand on the balcony at dusk and watch the cars ride past, headed wherever is next. I do a lot of thinkin', but that don't mean I get around to a lot of knowin' always. But at least I'm thinkin'. I'm still sorry I ain't get to be the tree in the neighborhood that Quila wanted to plant. But I guess sometimes people get named wrong.

Acknowledgements

Much love and many thanks to:

Mandela Wise, Matt Herndon & Custom Graphics Atlanta, TEAM, NiQ and Jakyll, P. Lane and Pop, Jamal, Prati, Bosh, Ta'Nehisi Coates, Rupi Kaur, Doug Fletcher, Mr. Agnew and the Kindezi Schools, Mama Jenet, Graves Elementary, J.K. Rowling, the late, great Langston Hughes, Tarell Alvin McCraney, Barry Jenkins, Diijon DaCosta and the Dekalb County School District, Tamar Cantwell, Chris Wade, Edgar Varela, and the whole PiDD.

and especially:

Charli McCall, Daisha "Mouse" Hunter, Olivia, RMF Tiff, Sophia, Nneka, Kierra Wooden, Gabrielle Hickmon, Nabila Lovelace, Adrianna Cherelle, Kaija, Jalessah, Ms. Tassili, Cake, Kaci Diane, Ms. Vanzant, Laini, Tau Theta chapter of Zeta Phi Beta Sorority, Inc., Roxane Gay, Angie Thomas, Assata Shakur, Ava Duvernay, Zahni, Neka, Roe Freeman, LaShanna Stephens, Katie Mitchell, Chicago Char, Sharamie Elease, Kat, DIVAS Mentoring, and all the other phenomenal black women that have inspired me on this journey, and who inspire and make so many of us that much better each day. Thank you.

H.D. Hunter

is a writer and activist from Atlanta, GA. He holds a Bachelor's degree in English and a Master's in Business Management. More than he is a writer, he is a reader. More than he is an artist, he is a fan of art. He loves his sister, his friends, words, natural light and vegan food. He loves Love. In between the rising and setting of each sun, he seeks to do three things: help people, spread positivity, and create. You can find him and his work online at thesoutherndistrict.com and on social media @hd_tsd.